To my aunt Ann, the most thoughtful person I know

Love, Michael

To my parents

—I.F.

Dial Books for Young Readers
An imprint of Penguin Random House LLC, New York

First published in the United States of America by Dial Books for Young Readers,
an imprint of Penguin Random House LLC, 2021

Text copyright © 2021 by Michael Arndt • Illustrations copyright © 2021 by Irena Freitas

Visit us online at penguinrandomhouse.com.

Library of Congress Cataloging-in-Publication Data is available.

Manufactured in China
ISBN 9781984814364

10 9 8 7 6 5 4 3 2 1

Design by Mina Chung • Text set in Biko

Thoughts Are Air

by Michael Arndt

illustrated by

Irena Freitas

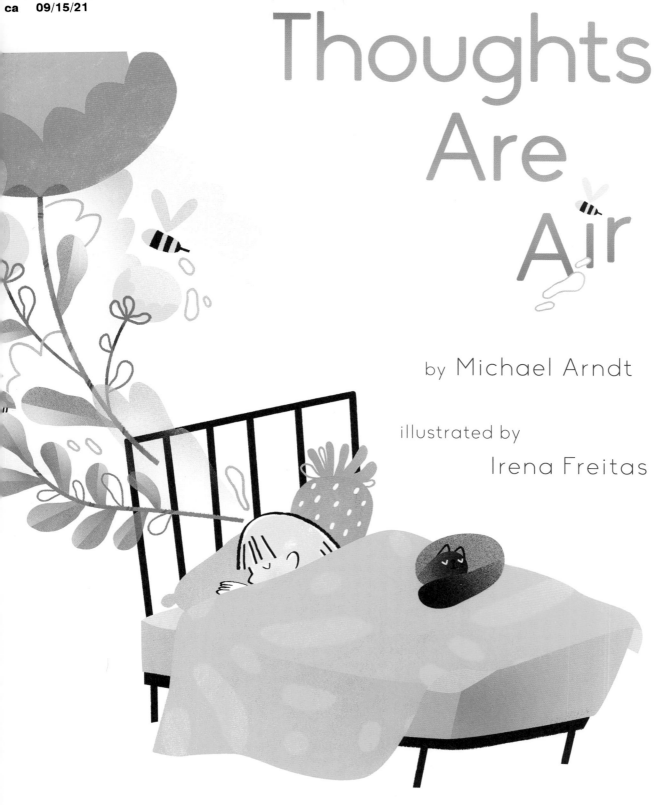

 Dial Books for Young Readers

Thoughts are air,
      clouds in your head
Dreams that you dream
      snug in your bed.

Thoughts are feelings,
breezes that sway
Touching your heart
then fading away.

Thoughts are beliefs,
winds that inspire
When you feel low
they lift you up higher.

Thoughts are ideas,
    steam for your plans
Big, bright balloons
    to faraway lands.

Thoughts are breaths,
the ones you express

Thoughts become words
so please think your best.

Words are water,
an underground spring
Your voice flowing forth
when you write,
speak, or sing.

Words are letters,
        wells of wet ink
Shapes that you draw
        to show what you think.

Words are sounds,
   waves that you hear
Tides that roll in
   and out of your ear.

Words are meaning,
oceans so deep
Reflecting the truth
while secrets they keep.

Words are power,
    in so many ways
Words become actions
    when you do what you say.

Actions are earth,
volcanos that hold
the fire inside you
to get up and go.

Actions are work,
    hills that you hike
Work can be fun
    when it's something you like.

Actions are plots,
the soil you sow
What you care for
is what you will grow.

Actions are deeds,
        bricks you stack tall
What will you build . . .
        a bridge or a wall?

Actions are matter,
     thoughts that came true
Actions are words
          you decided to do.

Thoughts are memories,
          actions now past
Words you reread
          from first page to last.